The Very Special CHRISTMAS

Christine Leeson

Illustrated by Gaby Hansen

LITTLE TIGER PRESS

It was Molly Mouse's first Christmas. The sky was streaked with pink and gold, and there was a tingle in the air.

Through the window of a house something was shining and glittering into the night.

"What is that, Mom?" asked Molly.

"It's a Christmas tree," said her mother. "People cover it with shiny balls, lights, and stars."

"I wish *we* had a Christmas tree," sighed Molly.

"Why don't you go into the woods to find one?" said her mother. "You could make it look just as nice as that tree in the window."

Molly thought this was a great idea.
She called her brothers and sisters together,
and off they all scampered.

On the way to the woods, they came to a barn.
The mice rummaged through it, looking for
something to add to their tree. Under a big
pile of hay, Molly found a doll.
   "This is like the doll on the top of the
Christmas tree in the window," she said.
"It will be just right for our tree."

But the doll belonged to someone else.

"Grr!" said the old farm dog. "That's mine!"

"Don't chase us!" cried Molly. "I only thought the doll would look nice on our Christmas tree."

The old dog yawned. It was true that sometimes he chased mice. But because it was Christmas, or because he remembered the Christmas tree in the farmhouse and how he used to play with the children there, he said the mice could borrow the doll.

The mice left the barn and walked across
the barnyard, carrying the doll. They came
to the edge of the woods.

"Hey," Molly shouted. "I see something
else we can put on our Christmas tree!"
It was a gold ribbon, hanging from a
branch of an oak tree. Molly scampered
up the trunk, took hold of the ribbon,
and pulled . . . .

But the ribbon belonged to a magpie.
She had taken it to line her nest.
"Please don't be angry," said Molly.
"I only wanted the gold ribbon for
our Christmas tree."

Usually the magpie chased mice. But because
it was Christmas, or because she had been
admiring the Christmas tree in the window, she
let go of the other end of the ribbon. Molly took
the ribbon thankfully.

In the distance Molly saw some shiny round things lying on the ground. They were like the shiny balls on the Christmas tree in the window.

"Exactly what we want!" cried Molly, running to pick one of them up. "Now we have a doll, a gold ribbon, and a shiny ball!"

But those shiny balls belonged to a fox. "Those are my crab apples," he barked. "I'm saving them for the cold days ahead."

"We only thought one would look good on our Christmas tree," said Molly, trembling.

The fox sniffed. He chased mice most of the time. But because it was Christmas, or because he had never seen a Christmas tree before, he went back into the woods. Molly picked up a shiny crab apple and carried it away.

Twilight was falling as the mice
went deeper into the woods.

At last, in a clearing, they found
a large evergreen tree.

"Our Christmas tree!" cried Molly.

On its branches they hung the doll,
the ribbon, and the crab apple.

"Oh," said Molly when they had finished.
"It doesn't look like the tree I saw."
Sadly the mice turned away and, disappointed,
went all the way home to bed.

In the middle of the night Mother Mouse
woke up Molly and her brothers and sisters.
   "Come with me," she whispered. "I have
something to show you."
   The mice scurried along
behind their mother,
into the woods.
Sometimes other
animals hurried
on ahead
of them.

At last the mice reached
the clearing. Molly stood
completely still. Her eyes
grew large and round.
   "Oh, look at that!"
she cried.

During the night the animals had all added more decorations to the Christmas tree, and the snow had come and touched everything with glitter. The little tree twinkled brightly in the darkness.

"Our tree is even better than the one in the window," whispered Molly, happily.

And because it was Christmas, all the animals sat quietly around the tree, at peace with each other.